The Boy AND the Tigers

By Helen Bannerman
Illustrated by Valeria Petrone

🔖 A GOLDEN BOOK · NEW YORK

Copyright © 2004 by Random House, Inc. All rights reserved under International and Pan-American Copyright Conventions. Published in the United States by Golden Books, an imprint of Random House Children's Books, a division of Random House, Inc., New York, and simultaneously in Canada by Random House of Canada Limited, Toronto. Golden Books, A Golden Book, A Little Golden Book, the G colophon, and the distinctive gold spine are registered trademarks of Random House, Inc. Library of Congress Control Number: 2003104577
ISBN: 978-0-375-82719-8
www.goldenbooks.com
Printed in the United States of America   First Random House Edition 2004
20 19 18 17 16 15 14

Helen Bannerman, an Englishwoman who lived in India for thirty years, made up The Story of Little Black Sambo for her two daughters on a long train ride in 1899. For this edition of Bannerman's story, the little boy and his parents have been given new names.

Once upon a time there was a little boy, and his name was Little Rajani. And his Mother was called Ramita. And his Father was called Kapaali. And Ramita made him a beautiful little Red Coat, and a pair of beautiful little Blue Trousers.

And Kapaali went to the Bazaar, and bought him a beautiful Green Umbrella, and a lovely little pair of Purple Shoes with Crimson Soles and Crimson Linings.

And then wasn't Little Rajani grand? So he put on all his Fine Clothes, and went out for a walk in the Jungle. And by and by he met a Tiger.

And the Tiger said to him, "Little Rajani, I'm going to eat you up!"

And Little Rajani said, "Oh! Please, Mr. Tiger, don't eat me up, and I'll give you my beautiful little Red Coat."

So the Tiger said, "Very well, I won't eat you this time, but you must give me your beautiful little Red Coat."

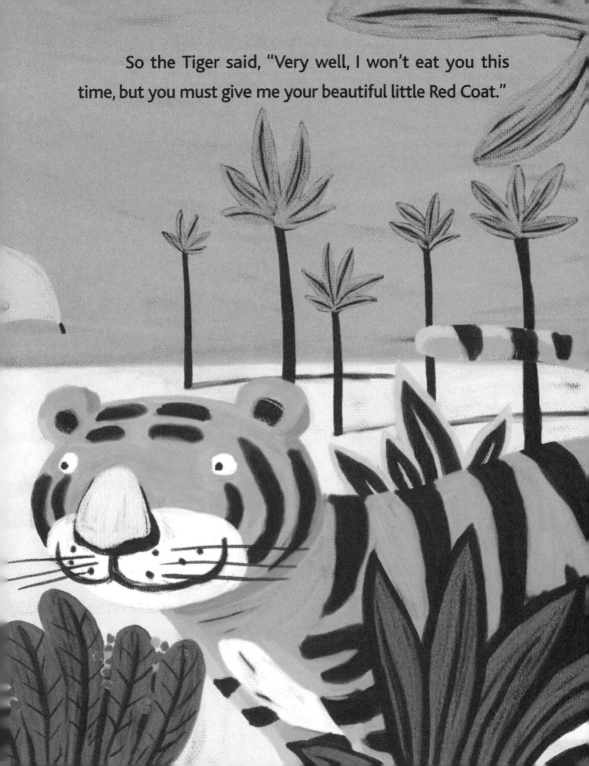

So the Tiger got poor Little Rajani's beautiful little Red Coat, and went away saying, "Now I'm the grandest Tiger in the Jungle."

And Little Rajani went on, and by and by he met another Tiger, and it said to him, "Little Rajani, I'm going to eat you up!"

And Little Rajani said, "Oh! Please, Mr. Tiger, don't eat me up, and I'll give you my beautiful little Blue Trousers."

So the Tiger said, "Very well, I won't eat you this time, but you must give me your beautiful little Blue Trousers."

So the Tiger got poor Little Rajani's beautiful little Blue Trousers, and went away saying, "Now *I'm* the grandest Tiger in the Jungle."

And Little Rajani went on and by and by he met another Tiger, and it said to him, "Little Rajani, I'm going to eat you up!"

And Little Rajani said, "Oh! Please, Mr. Tiger, don't eat me up, and I'll give you my beautiful little Purple Shoes with Crimson Soles and Crimson Linings."

But the Tiger said, "What use would your shoes be to me? I've got four feet, and you've got only two; you haven't got enough shoes for me."

But Little Rajani said, "You could wear them on your ears."

"So I could," said the Tiger, "that's a very good idea. Give them to me, and I won't eat you this time."

So the Tiger got poor Little Rajani's beautiful little Purple Shoes with Crimson Soles and Crimson Linings, and went away saying, "Now *I'm* the grandest Tiger in the Jungle."

And by and by Little Rajani met another Tiger, and it said to him, "Little Rajani, I'm going to eat you up!"

And Little Rajani said, "Oh! Please, Mr. Tiger, don't
eat me up, and I'll give you my beautiful Green Umbrella."

But the Tiger said, "How can I carry an umbrella,
when I need all my paws for walking with?"

"You could tie a knot on your tail and carry it
that way," said Little Rajani.

"So I could," said the Tiger. "Give it to me, and I
won't eat you this time."

So he got poor Little Rajani's beautiful Green Umbrella, and went away saying, "Now *I'm* the grandest Tiger in the Jungle."

And poor Little Rajani went away crying, because the cruel Tigers had taken all his fine clothes.

Presently he heard a horrible noise that sounded like "Gr-r-r-r-r-rrrrrrr," and it got louder and louder. "Oh! Dear!" said Little Rajani. "There are all the Tigers coming back to eat me up! What shall I do?"

So he ran quickly to a palm tree, and peeped round it to see what the matter was.

And there he saw all the Tigers' fighting, and disputing which of them was the grandest. And at last they all got so angry that they jumped up and took off all the fine clothes, and began to tear each other with their claws, and bite each other with their great big white teeth.

And they came rolling and tumbling right to the foot of the very tree where Little Rajani was hiding, but he jumped quickly in behind the umbrella. And the Tigers all caught hold of each other's tails, as they wrangled and scrambled, and so they found themselves in a ring round the tree.

Then, when the Tigers were very wee and very far away, Little Rajani jumped up, and called out, "Oh! Tigers! Why have you taken off all your nice clothes? Don't you want them anymore?"

But the Tigers only answered, "Gr-r-rrrr!"

Then Little Rajani said, "If you want them, say so, or I'll take them away."

But the Tigers would not let go of each other's tails, and so they could only say, "Gr-r-r-r-rrrrrr!"

So Little Rajani put on all his fine clothes again
and walked off. And the Tigers were very, very angry,
but still they would not let go of each other's tails.

And they were so angry that they ran round the tree, trying to eat each other up, and they ran faster and faster, till they were whirling round so fast that you couldn't see their legs at all.

And they still ran faster and faster and faster, till they all just melted away, and there was nothing left but a great big pool of melted butter (or *ghi*, as it is called in India) round the foot of the tree.

Now, Kapaali was just coming home from his work, with a great big brass pot in his arms, and when he saw what was left of all the Tigers he said, "Oh! What lovely melted butter! I'll take that home to Ramita for her to cook with."

So he put it all into the great big brass pot, and took it home to Ramita to cook with.

When Ramita saw the melted butter, wasn't she pleased! "Now," said she, "we'll all have pancakes for supper!"

So she got flour and eggs and milk and sugar and butter, and she made a huge big plate of the most lovely pancakes. And she fried them in the melted butter which the Tigers had made, and they were just as yellow and brown as little Tigers.

And then they all sat down to supper. And Ramita ate Twenty-seven pancakes, and Kapaali ate Fifty-five, but Little Rajani ate a Hundred and Sixty-nine, because he was so hungry.